STORIES FOR 6 YEAR OLDS

GW01091080

A Random House book
Published by Random House Australia Pty Ltd
Level 3, 100 Pacific Highway, North Sydney NSW 2060
www.randomhouse.com.au

First published by Random House Australia in 2005
This edition published in 2011

Text copyright © see acknowledgements for individual stories
Illustrations © Jobi Murphy 2005

Addresses for companies within the Random House Group can be found at
www.randomhouse.com.au/offices.

National Library of Australia
Cataloguing-in-Publication Entry

Stories for six year olds.

Includes index.
For children aged 5–6 years.

ISBN 978 1 74275 371 3

1. Children's stories, Australian. I, Knight, Linsay, 1952–.

A823.01089282

Cover and text design by Jobi Murphy
Illustrations by Jobi Murphy
Typeset in Futura (junior)
Printed in Australia by Griffin Press, an Accredited ISO AS/NZS 14001:2004
Environmental Management System printer.

STORIES FOR 6 YEAR OLDS

Edited by Linsay Knight
Illustrated by Jobi Murphy

RANDOM HOUSE AUSTRALIA

Foreword

BY POPULAR DEMAND!

Do you ever get asked to recommend stories suitable for six year olds or test new authors on children this age? Well, if you do and you need some help, your wait is over. Because *Stories for 6 Year Olds* is here!

For quite some time booksellers, parents and grandparents alike have been clamouring for a series with stories especially chosen to appeal to children of different ages. The first of these four eclectic collections features local Australian storytellers such as Margaret Clark, Duncan Ball, Jenny Wagner, Anna and Barbara Fienberg, Victor Kelleher, Clare Scott-Mitchell, Gretel Killeen and Kim Caraher, as well as international contributors such as Malorie Blackman and Joan Aiken.

The stories for each age group have been selected by Children's anthologist and publisher, Linsay Knight, and she has tailored them to suit the interests and reading abilities of young readers as, year by year, they gain in confidence and want to be extended. The illustrator and designer of the series is Jobi Murphy and she has taken reading requirements, such as ratio of text to illustration and the type size, into account when putting the books together.

Short, clearly displayed texts are designed for reading along with a six year old or to inspire confidence in a child who wants to read to an adult or older child. Black-line illustrations spread throughout help put the story in context and add visual clues. The familiar world of stories and characters is important at this level. Beginner readers enjoy finding characters like themselves, their friends and their pets in these books – and in this familiar world they also encounter the unexpected. While the language will be familiar, the introduction of some new words in familiar contexts also helps build vocabulary.

This book looks friendly and accessible and is a must for children who like to be read to or who want a good read.

Contents

The Biggest Boast

MARGARET CLARK

It was strange going to a new school. Ben stood in the playground and hoped someone would talk to him.

He munched his apple and tried to look casual and cool.

That kid looks tough. That kid looks rough. And that one looks awesome! I hope

they're friendly, he thought.

'Hey. You. New kid. What's your name?' It was the tough one. He walked over to Ben. The rough one and the awesome one came too. He was surrounded.

'Ben,' he said.

'Ben? Ben the Hen?

Ben the Pig Pen?'

Ben kept quiet and waited to see what would happen next.

'Leave him alone,' said a voice.

It was a girl with long hair in a ponytail and mega freckles. She grabbed Ben by the arm and steered him away. Ben felt stupid at being rescued by a girl.

He shook his arm free.

'Wait,' said Ben, changing his mind. Perhaps it was better to have a friend who was a girl than no friend at all.

Sally didn't have a friend. Ben didn't have a friend. So it seemed a good idea to

spend time together. But Sally had one big fault. (Which was probably why she was not popular.)

She liked to boast.

'My house is the biggest in the whole of Smith Street,' she said. 'Number 123.'

'My house is the biggest in the town,' said Ben.

It was true, because Ben's father was

3

the new Town Clerk, so they were living in some rooms at the back of the City Hall until their new house was ready.

'Huh,' said Sally. 'My dog Delmonico has a pedigree a mile long and is related to royalty.'

'Huh, huh,' said Ben. 'My dog Gummlington the Third is one hundred and forty-nine years old and has no teeth.'

'Well, that's nothing,' said Sally. 'My dad is the smartest dad in the whole world. On Mondays he's an astronaut. He's getting ready for the first flight to Mars. Or Jupiter. Whichever he prefers.

'On Tuesdays he's a biker with the Foul and Filthy Motorbike Club.

'On Wednesdays he's a bank manager and counts all the money.

'On Thursdays he's an ambulance driver. He gives people the Kiss of Life.

'On Fridays he flies jumbo jets to foreign countries and back in time for tea.'

'That's a lie,' said Ben. 'You can't fly from China to Australia and back that quickly.'

'Haven't you heard of the International Date Line?' said Sally.

'Of course,' said Ben, who hadn't.

Ben thought quickly just as the bell rang to go back into school.

'Huh, huh, huh, huh, my dad's … my dad's the boss of this town, so there.'

But it didn't sound very important at all. When the class was doing Social Studies, Ben wrote Sally a note. It said:

What's your dad do on Saturdays
and Sundays, then? Mine is training
for the Olympics on Saturday.
He's running in a race.
And on Sunday, he's flying the world's
biggest kite with me in the park.

Back came a note from Sally:

My dad plays lead guitar with
the 'Dead Sea Scrolls' on
Saturdays. And on Sundays
he's the conductor of the
Melbourne Symphony Orchestra,
so I'm free on Sunday. Can I come
and watch you fly the world's
biggest kite?

Ben wrote back just as his teacher came to look at his work:

Sure.

But the teacher didn't see his note. That was a lucky break.

On Sunday there was a good, stiff breeze blowing when Ben and his dad went to the park. Gumbo went too. He liked to sniff the tree trunks and slobber on friendly people and roll upside down in the grass with his legs in the air.

There were lots of people flying kites, but Ben's was the biggest and the best. Together Dad and Ben had spent hours making it on cold, wintry nights. It was painted a fearsome red with big black writing, BEN AND DAD COMBO. The tail was black and blue, because Dad said that's the colour they'd both be when they bruised themselves crashing into trees, falling into lily ponds while they were flying the kite.

'Hi, Ben.'

It was Sally. She was holding a dog's lead with a very fat corgi on the end.

'Just like the Queen's,' said Ben, trying to be kind, because it really was a peculiar-looking dog. It looked like a brown and white ball on four stumpy legs.

Sally tied Delmonico to the bench with Gumbo, and Ben's dad showed her how to fly the kite.

After a while she was really good.

'Do you want to come home for some lunch?' said Dad.

When Sally said yes, Dad reminded her that they would have to check with her mum.

'She knows where I am,' said Sally, going very quiet. She had a strange look on her face.

'I'd like to meet her,' said Dad firmly. 'Where do you live, Sally?'

Sally seemed to have forgotten, but Ben remembered.

They walked back through the park and called in at Sally's on the way.

She did live in a very big house, but it was divided into eight separate flats.

When Dad knocked at the door her mum came out looking tired, with a toddler on one hip and another child clutching at the knees of her jeans. She offered to make them some ham rolls and coffee right there and then, so Ben was pleased, because he hated Dad's soggy egg sandwiches.

'Del, get off the sofa,' said Sally's mother. Del? thought Ben, as Sally's mum shooed the dogs into the garden.

There was a photo of a handsome man on the sideboard. Ben stared at it. The man looked like someone he knew. Sally.

'That's Sally's dad,' said her mum. 'He died last year.' Sally made a funny noise and rushed off into her bedroom.

But Ben didn't mind. He knew what it was like, because he didn't have a mum.

He followed her and knocked at her door.

'Hey,' he said. 'I've got the best collection of computer games in the whole world. Want to come over and play with them?'

So they did!

RARE PET
SPUNKY MONKEY

Emily and the Mystery of the Missing Pets

DUNCAN BALL

'Emily, I'm a secret agent from InterPet,' the woman said. 'We need your help.'

'InterPet?' Emily said. 'I've never heard of InterPet.'

'No one has, Emily. Well, only the people

who are in it. We look after the pets of the world. We make sure that they're all safe and well and that somebody loves them.'

'That's nice,' Emily said. 'But what's the problem?'

'Pets are disappearing, Emily.'

'We were talking about that at school today,' Emily said. 'Yesterday my teacher, Ms Plump, lost her little kitten, Huggums. Annabelle's dog, Piddles, also went missing. And Jonathan has lost Squishy, his jellyfish.'

'It's happening everywhere,' the agent said. 'We think we know who's doing it but we are not allowed to tell you. Not till you say you'll help.'

'Why do you need me?'

'Because you're small and your eyefinger might come in handy. Oops! I didn't mean to say that. I wasn't making a joke about your eyefinger.'

'It's okay,' Emily said, 'I say it myself.'

Emily looked over at her parents.

'Is it okay if I help?' she asked.

'It's up to you, Emily,' Mrs Eyefinger said. 'But maybe you should think about it.'

'Yes,' Emily agreed. 'I'll decide tomorrow.'

'I hope you say yes,' the secret agent said. 'We really need you. My name is Petulia Chaser, by the way. Just call me Pet. Pet Chaser. Here's my card.'

Emily kept thinking about the missing pets. She woke up in the middle of the night and looked over at Fluffy, her goldfish.

'I don't know what I'd do if someone took you, Fluffy,' she said.

The next morning she got the shock of her life. 'Fluffy!' she cried. 'Someone's stolen Fluffy!' Sure enough, Fluffy's bowl was gone. Emily looked out the open window.

'That does it!' she said. 'Whoever stole Fluffy made a big *big* mistake! Don't you worry, Fluffy, I'm going to find you!'

An hour later Emily was at InterPet headquarters. Petulia and the other secret agents were gathered around her.

'You'll have to do some very sneaky things, Emily,' the agent said. 'Secret agents get to do sneaky things that no one else gets to do. They should call us *sneakret* agents.'

'I know about being a secret agent,' Emily said. 'I've been one before.'

'We're going to make you look just like a

pet so that you'll be stolen too. You're going to be a monkey. Follow me.'

Soon Emily was putting on a monkey suit. But instead of a monkey head, a make-up artist put bits of rubber and hair and make-up on her face.

Then he held up a mirror.

'I'm a monkey!' Emily screamed. 'I'm just like a real monkey!'

'Yes, we've made a monkey out of you,' the agent said with a laugh. 'And a very good-looking monkey too. I think we'll call you a Spunky Monkey. Now get into this box.'

Emily climbed into a big wooden box. The agent closed the lid and wrote, 'RARE PET SPUNKY MONKEY' on it.

'The person stealing the pets is a woman named Joy Stikke,' the agent said.

'Joy Stikke?' Emily said. 'The really really rich lady who made computer games?'

'That's her. We had our eye on her but she suddenly disappeared. She's in a secret hideaway somewhere and you're going to lead us to her,' the agent said. 'First we're going to take you to a warehouse. Her helpers steal the pets and put them there. Then they're taken to the hideaway.'

'You could follow them.'

'Not a chance. This woman loves games. She knows all the tricks. Even our tricks. She's sneakier than the sneakiest sneakret agent. Do you know what this is?'

The woman held up a round piece of rubber.

'A plug for a bath tub?' Emily asked.

'Nope. It's a Screamy-Beeper.' The woman slid it into the glove of Emily's

monkey suit. 'It's right on the back of your hand. Press it when you get to the secret hideaway and we'll be on our way.'

When night came, the agents took Emily in her box to the warehouse where the pet stealers kept the stolen pets. They sneaked past the guards and put her in a room with lots of other pets in boxes.

'Good luck, Emily,' Agent Pet Chaser whispered before she crept away.

Emily poked her eyefinger through an air hole in the top of the box. She watched and waited.

17

Finally some people came. They put the pet boxes on a truck and drove them to a tiny airport. Soon Emily was on a plane, flying through the night. She could hear meows and woofs and a few tweets, squawks and splashes from the other boxes. She thought of Fluffy and wondered if he was there too.

The plane landed way out in a desert and stopped in front of an enormous rock.

'Hmm,' Emily thought. 'There's something strange about that rock.'

Sure enough the side of the rock opened and the plane went carefully inside. There was a huge *clong!* as the side of the rock closed tight again. Emily thought she remembered a secret rock hideaway just like this one in a computer game.

At one end of the huge hall sat a woman. Pets were running everywhere. Emily knew that the woman was the

computer games billionaire, Joy Stikke.

The boxes were taken out of the plane and placed on the floor.

'More pets!' the woman squealed. 'More beautiful pets! Oh, my dear sweet babies. Bring me a pet! Quick!'

Two men opened a box and took out a kitten.

'Hey, that's Ms Plump's kitten, Huggums!' Emily thought.

'Oh, you beautiful little thing,' the woman said, cuddling it. 'You are such a little darling. Oh, I love your little purr. Okay, that's enough of you. Get me another pet!'

This time it was a dog.

'That's Piddles!' Emily thought. 'Annabelle's dog!'

'Oh, little sweetums,' the woman said, letting the dog lick her cheek. 'You are wonderful. Okay, new pet! Hurry up, I'm bored!'

This time it was an aquarium. Emily knew right away whose pet it was.

'Poor Squishy,' she sighed. 'Jonathan would be so upset if he knew where his jellyfish was.'

Joy Stikke watched Squishy pumping his way back and forth, and then played with the other pets one by one. But there was no Fluffy and Emily was beginning to feel very sad. Where was he? The woman walked over to Emily's box.

'A Spunky Monkey,' she said. 'I've never heard of a Spunky Monkey. Let's see what you look like.'

The lid of the box opened and the woman lifted Emily out.

'You are a very good-looking monkey,' the woman said. 'Now do some monkey things for me.'

Emily leapt up and down and then ran in circles dragging her hands on the ground. She tried to do a back flip but landed on her bottom.

Nearby was a pole that went all the way up to the ceiling. Emily grabbed it and started to climb.

'*You* hopeless little thing,' the woman sighed. 'You're not even using your tail.'

Emily knew that her tail wasn't real. She couldn't swing by it. But she tried to swing by one arm.

'This is too hard,' she thought. 'I can't do

SCREAMY BEEPER

it. Gosh, I've forgotten about the Screamy-Beeper. I think it's time to squeeze it.'

Emily felt for the lump on the back of her hand but it wasn't there. Just then she felt something make its way down the sleeve of her monkey suit.

'Uh-oh,' she thought. 'It's slipped! Oh, no! It's tickling me under the arm!'

Emily was very ticklish and when anything was under her arm it made her giggle. She struggled to keep from laughing.

'There's something wrong with this monkey,' the woman said. 'It's twitching all over! It looks like it's going to throw up! Get the vet!'

Suddenly Emily burst out laughing. 'Now, hang on,' the woman said. 'Monkeys don't laugh.'

She grabbed Emily and started pulling off the monkey make-up from her face. Then she ripped Emily's monkey suit until it lay in shreds on the floor. There was Emily standing in her jeans and T-shirt.

'You're not a monkey!' Joy Stikke boomed. 'You're nothing but a little girl! You came to spy on me, didn't you? You're working for InterPet, aren't you?'

'I'm not allowed to tell,' Emily said.

'Well, you're my prisoner now, you little scamp! Lock her up, boys!'

Two huge men grabbed Emily.

'Wait!' Emily said. 'Tell me why you're stealing all these pets.'

For a moment Joy Stikke just stared at Emily. Then Emily saw tears forming in the woman's eyes.

'My parents wouldn't let me have a pet,' she sniffed. 'I kept asking but they wouldn't give me one. They said pets made them sneeze. I'll bet you have a pet.'

'I used to,' Emily said. 'I had a goldfish named Fluffy but your helpers stole him.'

'That's a lie! I told them never to steal goldfish. I hate goldfish! They're stupid. They just swim around and look ... fishy.'

'So who took him?' Emily asked. She was beginning to think she'd never see Fluffy again. She sniffed a little sniff and wiped her nose on her T-shirt.

'I loved Fluffy,' she said. 'And he loved me too.'

'Stop it!' the woman yelled. 'Stop looking sad. I hate that. You look the way I did when my parents told me I couldn't have a pet. Now I'm going to have every pet in the whole wide world! Yesssssssssss!'

'But how about the people you take them from? How do you think they feel about losing their pets?'

'Who cares? They can get new pets — and then I'll steal them too! Ha ha ha ha ha.'

Emily noticed the Screamy-Beeper lying on the floor nearby.

'Well, I think you're cruel and mean and nasty,' Emily said. 'And you're going to get caught.'

Emily made a dive for the Beeper but Joy Stikke snatched it first.

'Ah-hah! A bath plug! Why do you have this?'

'It's a ... it's a ... *lucky* bath plug.'

'Well, it isn't very lucky for you now, is it?' the woman laughed.

'Can I have my lucky plug back?' Emily asked. 'Please?'

'Is it really lucky?'

'Yes,' Emily said, suddenly having a very clever idea. 'I'll show you how lucky it is. Put it in one of your hands. If I guess which hand it's in then I get it back, okay?'

'Okay,' the woman said. 'Only you have to guess it right ten times in a row.'

Emily thought for a moment.

'Okay,' she said.

The woman put her hands behind her back and then put both fists out towards Emily.

'Which hand is it in?'

Emily had curled her own fingers in so

the woman wouldn't see her eyefinger. Now she put her hands out towards the woman's.

'What are you doing?'

'I have to be near it for it to be lucky,' Emily said. 'Don't worry I won't touch your hands.'

Emily made her hands go round and round the woman's. And when they were under the woman's fists she secretly looked up with her eyefinger. The Screamy-Beeper was just big enough for her to see it between the woman's fingers.

'It's in your right hand,' Emily said.

The woman opened both hands.

'That was lucky,' the woman said.

'That's what I told you,' Emily said. 'It's lucky every time.'

Once again, the woman hid the Scream-Beeper and once again Emily found it. Again and again she found it until it was the tenth time.

'Now this time you have to give it to me

if I get it right,' Emily said. 'That was the deal.'

The woman hid the Beeper again and once again Emily got it right.

'See how lucky it is?' Emily said. 'Okay, give it to me.'

'No.'

'But you promised.'

'I don't trust you, little girl. You tricked me. And you're a sneak.'

'Okay, so I am a sneak,' Emily said. 'Sometimes we have to do sneaky things — like this!'

With this, Emily held her eyefinger right up to the woman's face. There was shock in the woman's eyes.

'Good grief!' she screamed. 'An eye on a finger! That's horrible!'

The moment she screamed, Emily grabbed the Beeper out of her hands and pressed the button in the middle. There was no sound but Emily could feel it wiggling back and forth.

Soon there was a huge crash as the door fell in. The InterPet secret agents rounded up Joy Stikke and her helpers.

'You did a great job!' Agent Pet Chaser said. 'Everyone will get their pets back again and will be very happy.'

'I'm just happy that I could help,' Emily said. 'But where's Fluffy, my goldfish? She said she didn't take him.'

'She didn't,' the agent said. 'I took him. Don't worry, he's back in your house now, safe and well. You see, we really needed your help. We thought you'd help us if he went missing.'

'Shame on you,' Emily said, with a little smile. 'That was a very sneaky thing to do.'

'As I told you,' the woman said, 'we secret agents have to do sneaky things sometimes.'

The Old Duppy's Curse
Or How I Was Turned into
a Crocodile!

MALORIE BLACKMAN

Part One

'If you walk through a puddle,
You'll get into trouble,'
My mother said to me.
When I asked her, 'Why?'
She said with a sigh,
'Because I said so! See!'

But that night in bed,
I hugged Mum and said,
'If I ask you something, don't shout.
It's just that this morning
You gave me a warning.
Please tell me what that was about.

I still do not get
Why my socks can't get wet.'
Mum said, 'Jean, it's something
    much worse.
It's something so evil
It's hard to believe ...
It's the fault of the old duppy's curse.

'See, when I was nine,
I thought it was fine
When off to see Gran I was sent.
She gave us the airfare,
Told us how to get there,
So off to Barbados we went!

'It's a very sad story
And one that I'm sorry
To say has just me to blame.
For by my gran's barn
And causing no harm
Lived a duppy, with eyes of red flame.'

33

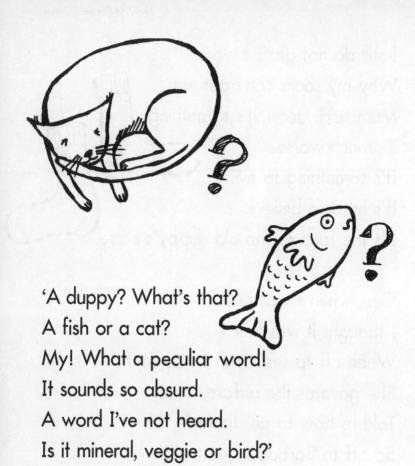

'A duppy? What's that?
A fish or a cat?
My! What a peculiar word!
It sounds so absurd.
A word I've not heard.
Is it mineral, veggie or bird?'

'Duppies are ghosts
That stay with their hosts
And scare all the neighbours away.
They say to be free
That water's the key,
It's water that keeps them at bay.

'So one night I sneaked out,
There was no-one about,
And the moon was up high in the sky.
I went to our well
(It's a sad tale to tell,
But I'm not going to tell you a lie).

'I filled up my pail,
Sure that I couldn't fail,
And up to the barn on tiptoe
I silently crept.
As the poor duppy slept
I circled him, silent and slow.

'Over the duppy
I then held my bucket
And with a great flourish I said,
    "Mr Duppy it's me!
You are now history!"
And I dumped the
    whole lot on his head!

'The furious duppy
Rose up high above me
And pointing his finger he growled,
"As you're so fond of water,
When you have a daughter ..."
He paused as the wind
    moaned and howled.

'"When you have a child,
Of her you'll be proud,
But she'd better stay out of the rain.
If she goes through a puddle
She'll be in BIG trouble,
And you'll be the person to blame.

'"Her face will start changing,
Her limbs rearranging,
She'll change right before you, and then,
You won't recognise her.
In fact you'll despise her.
And you won't see her true face again ..."

'And that is why, Jean,
It's not me being mean,
Please believe what I'm saying to you.
You mustn't go wading,
Or else I'm afraid
That the old duppy's curse will come true.'

Then Mum tucked me in,
Kissed my forehead, my chin.
And she patted my hands and my head.
She switched off my light,
Saying, 'Sleep well. Good-night.'
But I dreamt of the duppy instead,
And the horrible things he had said.

Part Two

The very next day, it rained and it poured,
All day I'd been sitting down,
 terribly bored.
So when Mum arrived to get me
 from school,
I thought to myself, 'I shall test out
 Mum's rule!'

Deep down I had thought that my mum'd
 been joking,
So I danced along till Mum called me
 provoking.
I came to a puddle; before she could
 stop me,
I waded right through it — and that's
when it shocked me ...

When I'd started to wade,
    I had shoes on my feet.
And my socks were pulled up —
    all tidy and neat.
But when I came out, instead of each shoe,
I had massive CLAWS —
    it's perfectly true!

My teeth seemed to sprout from
    all over my head,
And as for my nose!
    What more can be said?
I looked in the puddle. I just couldn't smile.
There! My reflection! A huge crocodile!

I could see my reflection there in the water.
My body was fatter, more wrinkled
   and shorter.
My nostrils seemed metres away
   from my eyes,
And my teeth were a huge and
   inelegant size.

Gone was my beautiful brown
   and soft skin.
I'd knobbles without,
   and a tough hide within.
From out of my back I now grew a tail.
I wanted to howl and to shriek and to wail.

For I had been warned.

Yes, I had been told.

But I thought I was clever.

I thought I was bold.

And into the puddle I'd wanted to splash.

Now all I could do was to watch

people dash

To the left and the right of me.

No-one would stay.

With cries of

and

I shouted, 'Do something, Mum! Now!
    Do it quick!'
So she did. She said, 'Jean, serves you
    right — you're so thick!'
With her hands on her hips she said,
    'What did I say?
Suppose I can't help you and
    you're stuck that way?'

Mum was annoyed — that was
    quite plain to see
I thought to myself, 'Well, what about me!'
Mum said with a frown,
    'We'd better get home.
And when we get there,
    I'll get on the phone
And phone up Great-granny
    who lives on a farm
Away in Barbados. She'll help.
    There's no harm
In trying at any rate. Jean, you're so wild!

You're an exasperating,

IRRITATING
AGGRAVATING,

child!'

Mum said, 'Great-gran's wise and
    she'll help us for sure.
It's guaranteed that she can
    tell us the cure.
You've got to get home, Jean,
    that's what you must do,
Or else you may end up on show in a zoo.'
'It's not fair! I'm not moving,'
    I started to moan.
'Mum, couldn't you lift me
    and carry me home?'

Mum looked at me, scratched an ear,
    blinked an eye.

'You've got to be joking, Jean!'
   came her reply.
'But don't worry, darling,
   the duppy told lies.
Of course I still love you —
   in spite of your size!'
NEE! NAA! NEE! NAA!
   The sound filled my head.
'Why wasn't I changed to a rabbit instead?

'Oh Mum! Oh Mum!
   I can hear sirens wailing,'
I cried, my tail thrashing and threshing
   and flailing.
Above us a chopper,

its rotor-blades humming,
Called out on its speaker, 'Don't panic!
We're coming!'
'Run, Jean! You're short but there's
      no-one to match you!
For goodness sake, darling, please don't
      let them catch you!'
'I can't just go waddling right down
      the High Street!'
I said. 'What about all the people
      I'll meet?'

'We'll have to split up,
      we're too easy to spot.
They'll all think you'll eat me,
      as likely as not,'
Said my mum.
'Right!' I said. 'First, I'll get home on
      my own two — or rather — four feet.

'Mum, head off home and
   I'll be right, behind you.'
'OK, Jean,' Mum said. 'But please don't
   let them find you.'
I ducked round a corner and
   tucked in my bum,
Whilst the chopper above me
   continued to hum.
What could I do? Would I ever get home?
Never before had I felt so alone.
So afraid and so positive that I'd be spied.
There aren't many places a big croc
   can hide.

By some smelly old bins I ran into a cat.
It snarled, arched its back, bared its teeth
   and then spat.
A girl wearing glasses stepped right
   on my tail.
I started to howl and she started to wail.
I headed for home just as fast as I could.
(I shouldn't have bothered,
   it did little good!)

A man who was out with his dog had a fit.
I don't think he liked me —
   not one little bit.
He shivered, he quivered, he screamed
   and he shook.
And all of my powers of persuasion it took
To convince with my biggest
   and beamie smile
That I would *not* eat him.
   Not this crocodile!

47

I met with a team from the
    Six O'Clock News.
'You'll make a great wallet or a
    new pair of shoes!'
Said the journalist to me,
    but I'd had enough.
As if I would listen all day to such stuff.
The clouds had stopped raining.
    The sun had come out.
The streets were deserted,
    no-one was about.

At last I reached home.
    I hadn't been skiving,
But it still took an hour of
    ducking and diving.
For scorning Mum's warning,
    I felt such a twerp!
And being a reptile was *really* hard work!

Sam from next door
    came out and he saw me.
He called out, 'Mum! Mum!
    There's a crocodile. Look! See!'
Hands on her hips, her eyes wide
    with surprise,
She said, 'Samuel Wells! Don't you dare
    tell such lies.'

His mum wagged her finger and
    told him off more,
And just when I thought that she'd
    see me for sure
And scream, yell or chuck things or
    faint on the floor
My mum heard the racket and
    opened our door.

49

Part Three

'Hello there, Great-Grandma!'
   down the phone.
Mum shook her head and
   she started to moan.
'Don't shout in her ear, Jean! I'm deaf now!
   Good gracious!
Are you trying to yell all the way
   to Barbados?'

'Hello my dear! My fav'rite gran-chile!'
   said Great-granny.
'I hear that you're a ... crocodile.'

'Oh, yes I am, Gran, and I want to
    change back.
So please tell me how I should
    start to do that.'
'We're stuck, Gran,' Mum said,
    'that's why we called you.
Please help — 'cause we don't have a
    clue what to do!'

'Well, how did the poor gal
    get into this muddle?
You didn't allow her to wade
    through a puddle?'
'You've got it in one, Gran!'
    my mum shouted out.
'That's it in a nutshell,
    that's what it's about!'
'Ah! The old duppy's curse.
    So *that's* what's going on.
I'll check in my fact book. Wait there.
    Won't be long.'

'But Gran, we can't wait.
    The police are outside,'
Said my mum.
'Sorry, dear. Then you'll just have to hide.
I'll find out the cure just as soon as
    I'm able.
Till then, try the wardrobe or under
    the table.'
I shivered and shook, from my tail
    to my ears,
Whilst down from my eyes fell huge
    crocodile tears.
(Real ones!)

MEANWHILE, OUTSIDE THE HOUSE ...

'This is the police. We are here on all sides.
We know you are in there,
    so don't try to hide
Come out right this second.
    I've got lots of men.
Or we're coming in —
    I won't say it again!'

'Do hurry up, Gran ...'
    Mum said to the phone.
But the silence that answered showed
    we were alone.
'Please, Mum! Do something!'
    I shrieked in her ear.
'I'm trying to, darling.
    You just stay right there.'

'Hello? Can you hear me?
    Where's everyone gone?'
Mum gave a sigh as Gran yelled
    down the phone.
'We thought you'd got lost, Gran.'
    Mum pulled up a seat.
And what Granny said, well I just
    can't repeat!

'If my heart should fail, Gran,
    it's all on your head.
Speak a bit faster — *please!*'
    That's what Mum said.
'Umm-hhmm ... Yeah ... Yeah ...
    Oh, I see ...
'What ... ? Are you sure ... ?
    Why next to a tree ... ?
Umm ... Yep ... Oh, I understand ...
I just hope this works,
    'cause it sounds
    a weird plan ...

'Of course I believe you. No, I didn't say …
All right, Gran … all right, dear …
　　Well, have it your way.
'I'll phone you back after and
　　tell you the worst.
But we've got to go off now and
　　try it out first.
Gran, you're a marvel! An angel! A brick!
But goodness to gracious,
　　you get the hump quick!'

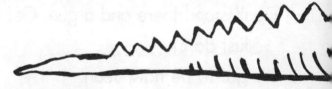

'What is it?' I asked her,
　　'I'm bursting to know.'
'Wait!' Mum said. 'Be quiet and
　　keep your voice low.'
So we ran through the kitchen,
　　afraid who we'd meet.
(My nose was so low,
　　I tripped over my feet.)

55

Mum said, 'Keep your eyes peeled
  and say if you see
A glistening puddle not far from a tree.'

We walked round the garden.
  I found one at last.
'Here's one, Mum, but hurry.
  It's drying up fast.'
'OK, Jean. Now you've got to
  walk backwards through it.
Don't stand there and argue. Get moving!
  Just do it!
It's got to be now, Jean.
  It's now or it's never.
Or else you may well be a reptile forever.'

So I shut my eyes tight and
  I did as Mum said.
My tail disappeared.
  Back came my true head.
Two legs and two arms.

And small, discrete teeth.
No knobbly bits with a
tough hide beneath.
Mum hugged me. I looked up at her
and I said,
'The next time it's raining,
I'm staying in bed!'

The Werewolf Knight

JENNY WAGNER

Feolf was a knight and a good friend of the king, but at other times he was a werewolf. That is to say, when the moon rose over the tops of the pine trees, Sir Feolf took off his fine woollen tunic and his cloak, hid them under a big rock, and turned into a wolf. All night long he would run in the forest, and when morning came he would change into a man again, get dressed and go home, and no-one was any the wiser.

Now a werewolf is a horrible beast to see, with his long fangs and his red tongue and his smoking breath, and Feolf was careful that no-one ever saw him in this state; for even as a wolf his heart was kind, and he did not want to frighten anyone.

And so it was that the Lady Fioran, who was Feolf's dearest friend, walked with him in the garden, and sat with him at dinner, and never once suspected there was anything amiss.

Fioran was the daughter of the king, and loved Feolf even more than her father did. When the king saw this he was greatly pleased, for Feolf and Fioran were the two he loved best in all the world. And when Feolf and Fioran decided to get married, the king was overjoyed.

To Feolf and Fioran

The king called for a feast that night, to mark the great event. The cups were filled with mead, the lords and ladies chattered, and the minstrels sang of great deeds long ago.

But before their song was ended, the moon rose. And Feolf slipped away to the forest and turned into a wolf

He did not come back till morning, and then Fioran found him walking in the garden. 'Where have you been, Feolf?' she asked.

But Feolf would not answer.

Then Fioran began to weep, for she was afraid he no longer loved her; and when Feolf saw this he was sorry, and told her his secret. Fioran was deeply troubled. She loved the knight very much, but it is a different thing to be married to a werewolf, and to tell the truth she was very much afraid. She imagined the wolf, with his gleaming eyes and his cruel teeth and his lolling tongue, and she dreaded marrying such a horrible beast.

And so she puzzled and grew more sad, and the wedding day drew closer and closer.

On the eve of her wedding day she went to the court magician and asked him what she should do.

'The answer is simple,' said the magician, who would have liked to marry Fioran himself. 'When Sir Feolf goes to the forest tonight he will hide his clothes under a rock. You must bring back his clothes and give them to me.'

'Is that all?' said Fioran. 'Just bring back his clothes?'

'Then all will be well,' said the magician.

That night, when Feolf slipped away to the forest, Fioran followed him. She brought back his clothes just as she was told and gave them to the magician.

When Feolf saw that his clothes were gone he pawed the ground and searched, and snuffed, and howled most piteously.

'Fioran!' he cried. 'Fioran!'

But a wolf does not have the gift of human speech, and only the crows in the pine trees heard him, and flapped their wings.

And so it was that Feolf did not come back to the castle that morning. For without his clothes he could not change back into human form, but must stay forever a wolf.

Far away in the castle, on her wedding day, Fioran waited. She put on her wedding dress and twined flowers in her hair, but Feolf did not come.

In the evening she went to the court magician. 'Where is he?' she asked. 'What has happened to him?'

'He was a werewolf,' said the magician. 'You are better off without him.'

Then Fioran shut herself in her room and wept for her lost knight, and no-one could comfort her; not the ladies of the court, nor the jesters, and not even the court magician, who kept sending her little presents.

The king was deeply saddened at the loss of his favourite knight, and decreed a time of mourning. There was no more feasting and no more dancing, and the minstrels hung their lutes on the wall.

Summer passed and autumn came, and Feolf stayed in the forest, living on wild roots and pine needles. The days grew colder and darker, and Feolf longed to be in the castle once again. He missed the feasting and the dancing, and he missed the warmth of his feather bed. But he missed Fioran most of all.

The king's sorrow grew as winter came, and one day his courtiers, trying to distract him, persuaded him to go hunting with them

in the forest. 'We might kill a bear,' they said. 'Or a wolf.'

And so one icy day the king rode out with his huntsmen and his hounds. Feolf heard the hunting horns from far off and laughed for joy, for he knew the king was coming; and he ran to meet his master, loping his wolfish lope and grinning his wolfish grin.

The huntsmen saw the wolf as he came on them in the clearing, but they did not know it was Feolf. They saw the horrible beast with his dripping jaws and his glittering eyes, and the nearest huntsman aimed his spear.

'Stop!' cried the king. 'Drop your spear!'

The huntsman dropped his spear, but he kept his eye on the wolf. 'Take care, sire,' he

said. 'A wolf is a savage beast, and should be killed before it does harm.'

But the king looked long at Feolf, and said, 'He is a sad wolf and I cannot find it in my heart to kill him. Take him back to the castle and give him food and find him a warm place to sleep.'

The huntsmen thought the king's long grief had turned his mind, and some would have killed the wolf then and there if they had not feared the king's anger. But they tied a rope round Feolf's neck, keeping well clear of his jaws, and started off for the castle.

When they drew near the castle Feolf lifted his head and sniffed; and then he bayed and howled with joy.

Fioran in her bedchamber heard it, and came running out in her dressing-gown, and ran to meet him and kissed him, and held his shaggy head between her hands and wept. Those who saw it were amazed, and all agreed that he was a very gentle wolf even a noble wolf, but no-one could tell the reason.

Fioran called the court magician and told him to bring Feolf's clothes. And before the astonished court Feolf put his clothes on and stood there once more as a noble knight.

The king was overjoyed to see Feolf again, the more so because Feolf had been loyal to him twice over; for even as a wolf he had been true to his king.

Then the king caused a feast to be set in the great hall, with dancing and merriment. The lutes were tuned again, the minstrels smoothed their throats with ale, and the ladies got out their dancing shoes.

Feolf and Fioran led the dancing that night, and when the moon rose Feolf did not go to the forest, but stayed with his bride. He had had enough of running wild in the forest, and from now on he was content to be just a man.

Only sometimes, when the night was particularly cold or the moon particularly bright, Feolf would slip away to the forest. But then Fioran kept a spare set of clothes for him, just in case.

The Patchwork Quilt

JOAN AIKEN

Far in the north, where the snow falls for three hundred days each year, and all the trees are Christmas trees, there was an old lady making patchwork. Her name was Mrs Noot. She had many, many little three-cornered pieces of cloth — boxes full and baskets full, bags full and bundles full, all the colours of the rainbow. There were red pieces and blue pieces, pink pieces and golden pieces. Some had flowers on, some were plain.

Mrs Noot sewed twelve pieces into a star. Then she sewed the stars together to make bigger stars. And then she sewed *those* together. She sewed them with gold thread and silver thread and white thread and black thread.

What do you suppose she was making?

She was making a quilt for the bed of her little grandson Nils. She had nearly finished. When she had put in the last star, little Nils would have the biggest and brightest and warmest and most beautiful quilt in the whole of the north country — perhaps in the whole world.

While his granny sewed, little Nils sat beside her and watched the way her needle flashed in and out of the coloured pieces, making little tiny stitches.

Sometimes he said, 'Is it nearly done, Granny?'

He had asked her this question every day for a year. Each time he asked it, Mrs Noot would sing:

'Moon and candle
Give me your light,
Fire in the hearth
Burn clear, burn bright.

'Needle fly swiftly,
Thread run fast,
Until the quilt
Is done at last.

'The finest quilt
That ever was,
Made from more than
A thousand stars!'

This was a magic song, to help her sew quickly. While she sang it little Nils would sit silent on his stool, stroking the bright colours of the quilt. And the fire would stop crackling to listen, and the wind would hush its blowing.

Now the quilt was nearly done. It would be ready in time for Nils's birthday.

Far, far to the south of Mrs Noot's cottage, in the hot, dry country where there is no grass and it rains only once every three years, a wizard lived in the desert. His name was Ali Beg.

Ali Beg was very lazy. All day he slept in the sun, lying on a magic carpet, while twelve camels stood round it, shading him. At night he went flying on his carpet. But even then the unhappy camels were not allowed to sit down. They had to stand in a square, each with a green lamp hanging on a chain round its neck, so that when Ali Beg came home he could see where to land in the dark.

The poor camels were tired out, and very hungry too, because they never had enough to eat.

As well as being unkind to his camels, Ali Beg was a thief. Everything he had was stolen — his clothes, his magic carpet, his camels, even the green lights on their necks. (They were really traffic lights; Ali Beg had stolen them from the city of Beirut one day as he flew over, so all the traffic had come to a stop.)

In a box Ali Beg kept a magic eye, which could see all the beautiful things everywhere in the world. Every night he looked into the eye and chose something new to steal.

One day when Ali Beg was lying fast asleep, the eldest of the camels said, 'Friends, I am faint with hunger. I must have something to eat.'

The youngest camel said, 'As there is no grass, let us eat the carpet.'

So they began to nibble the edge of the carpet. It was thick and soft and silky. They nibbled and nibbled, they munched and munched, until there was nothing left but the bit under Ali Beg.

When he woke up he was very angry.

'Wicked camels! You have ruined my carpet! I am going to beat you with my umbrella and you shall have no food for a year. Now I have all the trouble of finding another carpet.'

When he had beaten the camels, Ali Beg took his magic eye out of its box.

He said to it:

'Find me a carpet
Magic Eye,
To carry me far
And carry me high.'

Then he looked into the magic eye to see what he could see. The eye went dark, and then it went bright.

What Ali Beg could see then was the kitchen of Mrs Noot's cottage. There she sat, by her big fireplace, sewing away at the wonderful patchwork quilt.

'Aha!' said Ali Beg. 'I can see that is a magic quilt — just the thing for me.'

He jumped on what was left of the magic carpet. He had to sit astride, the way you do on a horse, because there was so little left.

'Carry me, carpet,
Carry me fast,
Through burning sun,
Through wintry blast.

'With never a slip
And never a tilt,
Carry me straight
To the magic quilt.'

The piece of carpet carried him up into the air. But it was so small that it could not go very fast. In fact it went so slowly that as it crept along, Ali Beg was burned black by the hot sun. Then, when he came to the cold north country where Mrs Noot lived, he was frozen by the cold.

By now night had fallen. The carpet was going slower and slower and slower — lower and lower and lower. At last it sank down on a mountain top. It was quite worn out. Ali Beg angrily stepped off and walked down the mountain to Mrs Noot's house.

He looked through the window. Little Nils was in bed fast asleep.

Tomorrow would be his birthday.

Mrs Noot had sat up late to finish the quilt. There was only one star left to put in. But she had fallen asleep in her chair, with the needle halfway through a patch.

Ali Beg softly lifted the latch. He tiptoed in.

Very, very gently, so as not to wake Mrs Noot, he pulled the beautiful red and blue and green and crimson and pink and gold quilt from under her hands. He never noticed the needle. Mrs Noot never woke up.

Ali Beg stole out of the door, carrying the quilt.

He spread it out on the snow. Even in the moonlight, its colours showed bright.

Ali Beg sat down on it. He said:

'By hill and dale,
Over forest and foam
Carry me safely,
Carry me home!'

Old Mrs Noot had stitched a lot of magic into the quilt as she sewed and sang. It was even better than the carpet. It rose up into the air and carried Ali Beg south, towards the hot country.

When Mrs Noot woke and found her beautiful quilt gone, she and little Nils hunted for it everywhere, but it was not in the kitchen — nor in the wood-shed — nor in the forest — nowhere. Although it was his birthday, little Nils cried all day.

Back in the desert, Ali Beg lay down on the quilt and went to sleep. The camels stood round, shading him.

Then the youngest camel said, 'Friends, I have been thinking. Why should we keep the sun off this wicked man while he sleeps on a soft quilt? Let us roll him onto the sand and sit on the quilt ourselves. Then we can make it take us away and leave him behind.'

Three camels took hold of Ali Beg's clothes with their teeth and pulled him off the quilt. Then they all sat on it in a ring, round the star-shaped hole in the middle. (Luckily it was a *very* big quilt.)

The eldest camel said:

'Beautiful quilt,
So fine and grand,
Carry us home
To your native land.'

At once the quilt rose up in the air, with all the camels sitting on it. At that moment, Ali Beg woke. He saw them up above him. With a shout of rage, he jumped up and made a grab for the quilt. His fingers just caught in the star-shaped hole. The quilt sailed along with Ali Beg hanging underneath.

The youngest camel said, 'Friends, let us get rid of Ali Beg. He is too heavy for this quilt.'

So all the camels humped and bumped and thumped, they knocked and rocked, they slipped and tipped, they wriggled and jiggled, until the needle which Mrs Noot had left sticking through a patch ran into Ali Beg's finger. He gave a yell and let go. He fell down and down, down and down and down, until he hit the sea with a great SPLASH!

And that was the end of Ali Beg.

But the quilt sailed on, with the camels. As they flew over Beirut, they threw down the twelve green traffic lights.

When at last they landed outside Mrs Noot's house, Nils came running out.

'Oh, Granny!' he cried. 'Come and see! The quilt has come back! And it has brought me twelve camels for a birthday present.'

'Dear me,' said Mrs Noot, 'I shall have to make them jackets, or they will find it too cold in these parts.'

So she made them beautiful patchwork jackets and gave them plenty of hot porridge to eat. The camels were very happy to have found such a kind home.

Mrs Noot sewed the last star into the patchwork and spread the quilt on Nils's bed.

'There,' she said. 'Now it's bedtime!'

Nils jumped into bed and lay proudly under his beautiful quilt. He went straight to sleep. And what wonderful dreams he had that night, and every night after, while his granny sat in front of the big fire, with six camels on either side of her.

Tashi and the Giants

ANNA FIENBERG AND
BARBARA FIENBERG

Jack ran all the way to school on Tuesday morning. He was so early, the streets were empty. Good. That meant he would have plenty of time to hear Tashi's new story.

Tashi was Jack's new friend. He'd come from a land far away, where he'd met fire-

breathing dragons and fearsome warlords. Today, Tashi had promised the story of Chintu, the giant.

Tashi was waiting for Jack on a seat by the cricket pitch.

'So,' said Jack, when he'd stopped puffing and they were sitting comfortably. 'Did you really meet a giant, Tashi?'

'Yes,' said Tashi. 'It was like this. Do you remember how I tricked the dragon, and put out his fire? Well, the dragon was furious, and he flew to the castle where his friend Chintu the giant lived. The dragon told him what I had done and Chintu boomed:

"FEE FIE FO FUM
I'LL CATCH THAT BOY FOR YOU,
BY GUM!"

'Chintu took one of his giant steps over to our village and hurled down great boulders, just as if they were bowling balls. Third Uncle's house was squashed flat as a fritter. Then the giant roared,

"*BRING TASHI OUT TO ME.*"

'The giant looked terrible standing there, so tall he cast a shadow over the whole village. He was as big as a mountain — imagine, a mountain that moved! — and tufts of hair stood up on his head like spiky trees.'

'So what did you do?' Jack shuddered.

'Well, it was like this. My father, who is a very brave man, ran out into the street and cried, "Be gone, Chintu, we will never give Tashi up to you!"

'The giant was quiet for a moment. Then he answered,

"*IF YOU DON'T BRING TASHI TO ME, I WILL COME BACK IN THE MORNING AND CRUSH EVERY HOUSE IN THE VILLAGE.*"

'The people all gathered in the square to discuss what to do. Some wanted to take me to the giant's house that night. Others were braver and said I should run away. While they were still arguing, I took the lantern and set out for Chintu's castle.

'I walked and walked until finally, there before me was the giant's castle, towering up to the sky. One path led up to a great door and windows filled with light, but another led down some winding stone steps.

'I took the lower path but the steps were so high I had to jump from each one as if

they were small cliffs. After a while I spied an arched wooden door. It wasn't locked and I pushed it open. It gave a groaning creak and a voice called out,

"Who's there? Is that you, Chintu, you fly-bitten lump of cowardly husband?"

'Now I saw a big stone-floored room and right in the middle was an enormous cage. Inside the cage was another giant.'

'Ooh!' said Jack. 'Two giants! Didn't you want to run?'

'No,' said Tashi. 'Not me. See, it was like this. The giant in the cage was sitting at a table eating some noodles. She was terrible to look at. She had only four teeth, yellow as sandstone, and the gaps in between were as big as caves.

'Well, while I was staring at her she said in a huge voice,

"Who are you?"

'So I told her that I was Tashi and what had happened and that I had come to persuade Chintu not to kill me. She gave a laugh like thunder and said,

"You won't change his mind easily, it sets like concrete. I should know, he is my husband! He tricked me into this cage and locked me up, all because we had an argument about the best way to make dumplings. He likes to grind bones for them, but I say flour is much better. Now Tashi, you need me to help you."'

'And she needed you to help *her*!' Jack said excitedly.

'Right,' said Tashi. 'So when she pointed to the keys over on a stool, I reached up and dragged them over to her. Mrs Chintu snatched them up and turned one in the lock.

"Now I'll show that lumbering worms-for-brains Chintu who is the cleverer of us two!"

'As she walked past, I scrambled up her skirts and hung on to her belt. She picked up a mighty club that was standing by the door and then she tiptoed to some stairs that led up and up through the middle of the castle.

'We came to a vast hall and there he was, sitting on a bench like a mountain bent in the middle. He was staring into the fire, bellowing a horrible song:

**"FEE FIE FO FOY,
TOMORROW I'LL GO AND
GET THAT BOY,
NO MATTER IF HE'S DEAD
OR JUMPING
I'LL GRIND HIS BONES TO
MAKE MY DUMPLING."'**

'Mrs Chintu crept up behind him, grabbed his tufty hair in one hand and held up the club with the other. I slid down her back to the floor.

'"Chintu, you pig-headed grump of a husband, I can escape from your cages, and make the best dumplings. Will you admit now that I am more that a match for you?"

'The giant rolled his great eyes and caught sight of me.

'"WHO IS THAT?" he roared.

'"That is the boy who chops our wood." And Mrs Chintu winked at me. "Now, let the boy decide who makes the best dumplings." She let go of Chintu's hair and gave me a hard look.

92

'"VERY WELL," Chintu said, and he rubbed his huge hands together.

'Later, they put some sacks down on the floor for me to sleep on. As he was going to bed, Chintu whispered — it was like a thunderclap in my ear — "IF YOU DECIDE THAT *HER* DUMPLINGS ARE BETTER, YOUR BONES WILL MAKE MY NEXT BATCH."

'And as his wife went by, she said, "If you decide that *his* dumplings are better, I'll chop you up for my next pot of soup."

'All night I walked up and down the stone floor, thinking what to do. And then I had one of my cunning ideas. I crept downstairs to the kitchen and had a good look about.'

'What were you looking for, Tashi?' asked Jack.

'Well,' said Tashi, 'it was like this. The next morning Mrs Chintu boiled her dumplings and then Chintu boiled his. When the dumplings were cooked they both spooned up one each, as big as footballs.

'"We must put a blindfold on the boy so he doesn't know which dumpling he is eating," said Mrs Chintu, and her husband tied a handkerchief over my eyes.

'I took a bite of one dumpling and swallowed it slowly. Then I tried the other. They watched me fiercely.

'When I had finished I said, "These are the best dumplings I ever tasted, and they are exactly the same."

'"NO THEY'RE NOT!" thundered Chintu.

94

"Taste them yourself and see," I said.

'So they did and they were very surprised.

'"The boy is right. They are the same," said Mrs Chintu. "And they are the best dumplings I ever tasted."

'So then I told them, "That's because I went downstairs last night and I mixed up the ground bones and the flour together. That's what makes the best dumplings — bones *and* flour."

'"What a clever Tashi," cried Mrs Chintu.

'"OHO! SO THAT'S WHO YOU ARE," bellowed Chintu, and he scooped me up in his great red hands. "I PROMISED MY FRIEND THE DRAGON THAT I WOULD SERVE YOU UP TO HIM IN A TASTY FRITTER THE NEXT TIME HE

CAME TO BREAKFAST."

'"Maybe so," said his wife, "but just try another dumpling first."

'The giant did, and when he had finished he thought for a minute. It was the longest minute of my life. Then the giant sighed and licked his lips. "DRAGON CAN HAVE A PLATE OF THESE DUMPLINGS INSTEAD," he said. "THEY ARE EXQUISITE. BE OFF WITH YOU NOW, TASHI."

'And so this time I walked out the great front door, as bold as you please. When I returned to the village they were still arguing about whether to give me up to Chintu or to let me run away. "I don't have to do either!" I cried, and I told them what had happened.

'"What a clever Tashi!" cried Grandmother.'

'So that's the end of the story,' said Jack sadly. 'And everyone was safe and happy again.'

'Yes,' said Tashi, 'that is, until the bandits arrived.'

The Bandits

One night Jack was reading a book with his father.

'This story reminds me of the time Tashi was captured by some bandits,' said Jack.

'Oh good, another Tashi story,' said Dad. 'I suppose Tashi finished up as the Bandit Chief.'

'No, he didn't,' said Jack. 'It was like this. One wet and windy night a band of robbers rode into Tashi's village. They were looking for some shelter for the night.

'But next morning, just as they were leaving, the wife of the Bandit Chief saw Tashi. He reminded her of her son, who had sailed away on a pirate ship, and she said to her husband, "That boy looks just like our son, Mo Chi. Let's take him with us."

'So Tashi was picked up and thrown on to one of the horses and away they went. He sneaked a good look about him, but he was surrounded by bandits, and it was impossible to escape. So Tashi had to think up one of his cunning plans.

'The first night when the bandits were still sitting around the fire after their dinner, the Bandit Chief said to Tashi, "Come, boy, sing us a song as Mo Chi did, of treasure and pirates and fish that shine like coins in the sea."

'Tashi saw that this was his chance. So what do you think he did?'

'Sang like a nightingale,' said Dad.

'**WRONG!**' said Jack. 'He sang like a crow. The bandits all covered their ears and the Bandit Wife said, "Stop, stop! You sing like a crow. You had better come over here and brush my hair like my son used to do." Tashi bowed politely but as he stepped around the fire, he filled the brush with thistles and burrs so that soon her hair was full of tangles.

'"Stop, stop!" cried the Bandit Wife, and her husband told her, "This boy is not like our son. He sings like a crow and he tangles your hair." Tashi put on a sorrowful face. "I will do better tomorrow," he promised.

'"You'd better," whispered the Chief's brother, Me Too, "or I'll boil you in snake oil."

'The next day when the bandits moved camp, they put all the rice into three big bags and gave them to Tashi to carry. When they came to a river, what do you think Tashi did?'

'Well,' said Dad, scratching his chin, 'he's such a clever boy, I expect he carried them over one by one, holding them up high.'

'**WRONG!**' said Jack. 'He dropped them all into the river. The bandits roared with rage. They called to Tashi to mind the horses. Then they jumped into the water and tried to recover the bags of rice that were sinking further down the river.'

'But Tashi reached them first, I suppose,' said Dad.

'No, he didn't,' said Jack, 'and when the bandits came back, all angry and dripping, they found that he had lost all the horses. The robbers began to whisper about the Bandit Wife, and Me Too gave Tashi evil looks. It took them a whole day to find the horses again.

'Well, that night, the Bandit Chief said to his wife, "This boy is not like our son. He sings like a crow, he tangles your hair, he loses the rice and scatters the horses." Tashi put on a sorrowful face. "I will do better tomorrow," he promised.

'"You'd better," whispered Me Too, "or I'll pluck out your nose hairs, one by one."

'On the third day, the bandits decided to attack the village where another band of robbers were staying. Just before dawn they quietly surrounded the camp — and what do you think Tashi did then?'

'He rode into the village and captured the chief,' guessed Dad.

'**WRONG!**' cried Jack. 'They were just preparing to attack, when Tashi accidentally let off his gun.

'The enemy was warned and Tashi's bandits had to gallop away for their lives.

When they were at a safe distance they stopped. The Chief's brother wanted to punish Tashi — he said he'd tie him up and smother him in honey and let man-eating ants loose upon him — but the Bandit Wife said, "No, let him come back to camp with me. He can help me roast the ducks we stole yesterday and we will have a feast ready for you when you return."

'So she and Tashi worked all day, plucking,

chopping and turning the ducks on the spit, and mouth-watering smells greeted the bandits as they drew near the camp that evening. And what do you think Tashi did then?'

'Washed his hands for dinner,' said Dad.

'**WRONG!**' said Jack. 'Just as the robbers jumped down from their horses, Tashi stumbled and knocked a big pot of cold water over the almost-cooked ducks and put out the fire.

"**ENOUGH!**" shouted the Bandit Chief to his wife. "This boy is not like our son. He sings like a crow, he tangles your hair, he loses the rice, he scatters the horses, he warns our enemies — and now he has

spoilt our dinner. This is too much." And he turned to Tashi. "You must go home to your village now, Tashi. You

are a clumsy, useless boy with no more brain than the ducks you ruined."

'Tashi smiled inside, but he put on a sorrowful face and turned to the Bandit Wife. "I'm sorry that I wasn't like your son," he said, but she was already on her way down to the river to fetch some more water.

'Tashi turned to go when a rough hand pulled him back.

"'You don't deserve to go free, Duck Spoiler," snarled Me Too. "Say goodbye to this world and hullo to the next because I'm going to make an end of you."

'But as he turned to pick up his deadly nose-hair plucker, Tashi shook himself free and tore off into the forest. He could hear

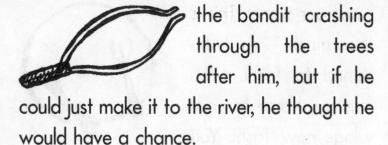 the bandit crashing through the trees after him, but if he could just make it to the river, he thought he would have a chance.

'He was almost there when he heard a splash. He looked up to see the Bandit Wife had slipped on a stone and had fallen into the water.

"HELP!" she cried when she saw Tashi. "Help me, I can't swim!"

'Tashi hesitated. He could ignore her, and dive in and swim away. But he couldn't leave her to drown, even though she was a bandit. So he swam over to her and pulled her ashore.

'By now all the bandits were lined up along the bank and the Chief ran up to Tashi. "Thank you, Tashi. I take back all those hard words I said about you. Fate did send you to us after all."

'Me Too groaned and gnashed his teeth.

'"Brother," said the Bandit Chief, "you can see Tashi safely home."

'"Oh no, thanks," said Tashi quickly, "I know the way," and he nipped off up the bank of the river, quicker than the wind.'

'So,' said Dad sadly, 'that's the end of the story and Tashi arrived safely back at his village.'

'WRONG!' said Jack. 'He did arrive back at the village and there were great celebrations. But at the end of the night, when everyone was going sleepily to bed, Third Uncle noticed that a ghost-light was shining in the forest.'

'And that's another Tashi story, I'll bet!' cried Dad.

'Right! said Jack. 'But we'll save it for dinner when Mum comes home.'

TASHI
...
to be
continued
...

Goblin in the Bush

VICTOR KELLEHER

Chapter One

Gibblewort was a nasty little goblin. He hated nearly everything. But most of all, he hated rainy weather.

Gibblewort lived in a country called Ireland, where it rains a lot, so he wasn't

very happy. One day he could stand it no longer. The walls of his treehouse were soggy, the floor all squelchy, and fungus was growing on the ceiling.

'If it rains again this week,' Gibblewort said crossly, 'I'm off to live in Australia.'

He had hardly spoken when he heard the swish of rain. So he bought a large green postbag and wrote this address on it:

AUSTRALIA
a nice dry part

Then he stuck on plenty of stamps, climbed inside the postbag, and pulled the flap closed.

He was so ugly and horrible that the other goblins were glad to post him off.

Chapter Two

He arrived in Australia one week later, still in his postbag. He was soon bumping along a dusty road on the back of a postie's truck. After a week inside the postbag Gibblewort felt grumpier than ever.

' **BLITHER and BLATHER!** '

he shouted. 'I'll not stay in here a minute longer!' And he kicked so hard that he rolled off the truck and landed on the road with a bump.

Gibblewort crawled from the bag groaning loudly. He didn't complain for long, though.

He looked about him with his beady eyes, and what he saw filled his heart with joy.

There wasn't a cloud in the sky. The earth and bush were as dry as straw. And the sun shone brighter than gold.

'This is the place for me,' he said. And he let out such a wicked chuckle that the birds stopped singing.

He danced a jig, and the insects stopped their scurrying. He grinned an evil grin, and the breeze stopped blowing.

'I'll soon show them who's boss around here,' he said. Then he sat down on a mound of earth to decide what his first bad deed would be. That same mound was a bull ant nest, and they didn't like anyone sitting on their roof. One of them rushed out and bit Gibblewort on his horny big toe.

'YEOW!'

he yelled. He leaped high in the air and landed back on the mound. The bull ants grew angrier still. Two more rushed out and nipped him on his ankles.

Gibblewort didn't understand what was happening. He seemed to be alone. Where were these sharp pains coming from?

'Show yourself and fight fair!' he screeched, dancing up and down.

But still no one appeared, and the biting got worse. That was when he decided that Australia must be haunted. By invisible ghosts that prodded you with red-hot needles.

For the first time in his horrid life Gibblewort took to his heels and ran.

Chapter Three

He was in an awful temper by the time he stopped for breath. He could hear a kookaburra cackling in a nearby tree.

'I'll teach you to laugh at me!' he shouted, and threw a stone at the bird. As the kookaburra flew off, an emu stepped from around the tree. Gibblewort had never seen a bird as big as this one. He thought the emu must be the kookaburra's mother, and he began to tremble with fear.

'I'm truly sorry, Mrs Bird,' he whined.

The emu was on the lookout for something to eat. She didn't know about goblins, so she walked over and pecked him on the ear.

'OW!'

said Gibblewort. He tried to run, but the emu was standing on his toe.

'OW-OW-OW!'

he said.

Luckily, the emu didn't like the taste of goblin and she soon moved off.

Gibblewort sighed. Free at last, he hopped away, holding his sore foot in one hand, his ear in the other.

Chapter Four

Gibblewort didn't stop to rest until he felt hot and tired. Hungry too. He licked his rubbery lips.

'What I wouldn't give for a bit of cooked rabbit.'

Just then his ears began to twitch. He could hear a rustle of leaves in the bushes.

'Could that be what I'm thinkin' it is?' he wondered.

'Munch! Munch!' Now he could hear the sound of munching.

'Yes, that'll be a rabbit,' he said with a nod.

Tiptoeing over to the bushes, he eased aside a leafy branch ... and nearly fainted! There before him stood the tall figure of a kangaroo. So close that its belly-fur tickled his nose. Far too close for Gibblewort's liking!

Gibblewort had already met the biggest bird in the world. Now here was the biggest rabbit.

'Heaven save me!' he cried.

But he should have kept quiet. His goblin voice startled the kangaroo. As it swung around to leap away, its long tail knocked Gibblewort head over heels.

Chapter Five

Gibblewort moaned as he rubbed his aching bones.

'They breed giant creatures here in

Australia,' he grumbled. 'What I need is something to beat them off with.'

He picked up a stick from the ground beside him. It looked just the thing. He hardly noticed its silky softness. What he did notice was how one end began to twitch. Next, the stick grew two staring eyes and a forked tongue. And then it hissed at him.

He felt his green goblin blood turn to ice.

'Is it giant worms now?' he croaked.

Dropping the snake, he scrambled up the nearest gum tree. Normally, that would have been the best thing to do, but a pair of magpies had chosen this tree for their nest.

Like the bull ants, they didn't want anyone near their home. Gibblewort most of all, with his red eyes and brown fangs and warty nose. He even had green moss growing under his nails!

He was halfway up the tree when the magpies dive-bombed him. Their jabs at his bald head didn't hurt him too much. A goblin's skull is harder than rock. But their pecking gave him such a shock, that he lost his hold and fell.

Gibblewort didn't hit the ground though. Something far worse happened. At that very moment an echidna walked past. Right beneath the tree!

Poor Gibblewort. He ran off faster than ever. Then he spent half an hour pulling out prickles from the tender parts of his body. For a while 'YIKES!' 'OUGH!' and 'OW!' were the only sounds to be heard.

Chapter Six

By now Gibblewort had begun to wish he'd never left Ireland. But goblins are stubborn creatures, and he wasn't ready to give up yet.

'At least I can find myself a nice dry home,' he said, trying to look on the bright side.

Ten minutes later, he spotted a wombat. It was digging in a sandy riverbed. Here at last was an animal Gibblewort had no need to fear. The wombat didn't bite him or peck him or tread on his toes. It just munched on a piece of root and hardly noticed he was there. Better still, it soon walked off.

The wombat left behind a beautiful hole. Deep and dark and dry, this was the home Gibblewort longed for.

He forgot about being hungry. He forgot about his bites and bruises. He crawled inside his new home and curled up.

'Aah, but it's grand to feel warm and

dry,' he said, and closed his eyes.

Like all goblins, Gibblewort slept soundly. That was why he didn't hear the rumble of thunder. He didn't see black clouds gather in the hills. Deep in his hole, he snored on while the rain fell. And he was still asleep when the flood came rushing down the riverbed.

As water filled his hole, he dreamed he was taking a bath. Now, goblins hate to wash their dirty bodies. Bath-time dreams are their worst nightmares. So imagine how Gibblewort felt when he awoke. When he found that his nightmare was real!

'HELP!'

he cried, and a green bubble popped from his mouth. 'I want to go home!' he wailed, and more bubbles followed.

They were noticed by a platypus. Always on the lookout for worms, the platypus swam down. Clamping its beak about the goblin's nose, it dragged him to the surface.

Gibblewort thought he'd been captured by a river monster.

'Leb go ob by doze,' he pleaded.

Like most Australian animals, the platypus was really a gentle creature. After giving Gibblewort's nose a last tweak — as if to say, 'What a pity this isn't a worm' — it swam off.

A very soggy Gibblewort was left to wade ashore.

Chapter Seven

He looked a sad sight as he limped up the bank.

'Oh, this Australia is a terrible place!' he wailed.

'It looks pretty good to me,' someone replied.

A young girl was smiling down at him.

'What do *you* know?' he said in a cross voice. 'Why, this Australia is full of ghosts and laughing birds and ... and giant creatures that'll eat you up, and ... and sticks that turn into devils, and ... and walkin' pin-cushions, and ... and floods and river monsters, and ... and I can't think what else!'

'I reckon you've had too much sun,' the girl said.

'**SUN!**'

screeched Gibblewort. 'It's the ugliest stuff in the whole world.'

'Well, you're not too good-looking yourself,' the girl told him.

She was sorry for her words a moment later when a big green tear rolled down the goblin's nose.

'All I'm really wantin',' Gibblewort sobbed, 'is to go home to rainy old Ireland.'

'Ireland?' the girl said. She pulled a large green postbag from behind her back. 'Is this yours, then?'

Gibblewort's face lit up. 'That's mine all right! You're a darlin' for findin' it.'

And he gave the girl a kiss. (It was the only kiss he ever gave anyone.) Then he crawled into the postbag and pulled the flap closed.

'Just send me back where I belong,' he called in a muffled voice.

So that's what the girl did. Partly because she felt sorry for him, and partly because she never wanted another goblin kiss.

Chapter Eight

Gibblewort arrived home during a heavy shower of rain.

He gazed fondly at his damp treehouse.

'Ah, this is the place for me,' he sighed.

The other goblins weren't too pleased to have him back. Yet he doesn't bother them much these days. Whenever he gets up to his nasty tricks, all they have to say is:

'Watch out! Or we'll pack you off to sunny Australia.'

Straight away Gibblewort hides under the bed and starts to shiver and shake.

Sleeping Beauty

Retold by

CLARE SCOTT-MITCHELL

A long time ago there lived a King and Queen. Every day they said to each other, 'If only we had a child!' But a child did not come.

One day when the Queen was in the bath, a frog came out of the water and

said, 'Your wish will come true. Before the end of the year you shall have a daughter.'

All that the frog had foretold came to pass. And in due course the Queen gave birth to a little girl. She was so lovely and the King was so happy that he wanted to have a great feast. He invited all his friends and relations, and he asked the wise women of the kingdom so that they would think well of the child, and always be kind to her.

Now, there were thirteen wise women, but the King had only twelve golden plates for them to eat off so one was not invited. The feast was very sumptuous and when it came to an end the wise women presented their magic gifts to the child. The first promised goodness, the second beauty, the third riches, and so on until there was very little else that the child could wish for.

When the eleventh wise woman had made her gift, a dark shadow fell across the door and the thirteenth burst into the room. She was shaking with rage because she had been left out and, pointing at the baby, she screamed, 'The King's daughter shall prick her finger on a spindle in her fifteenth year and fall down dead!'

And without another word she turned and left the room.

Everyone was shocked; but the twelfth wise woman, who had not yet presented her gift, came forward. 'I cannot altogether undo the wicked promise of the thirteenth wise woman, but I can soften it,' she said.

'The Princess shall not die in her fifteenth year, but when she pricks her finger she shall fall asleep for a hundred years.'

The King, who wanted to protect his child from harm, gave orders that every spindle in the kingdom should be burned. He sent men throughout the whole country, and they started fires that lit the sky throughout the long nights, as the spindles sputtered in the flames.

As she grew, the promised gifts of the eleven wise women were fulfilled. The Princess was good and beautiful, and kind and wise. Everybody who knew her loved her.

It happened that on the day of her fifteenth birthday, while the King and Queen were away from the castle, the Princess found a staircase that she had not seen before. She climbed up the stairs and heard a humming sound coming from behind a

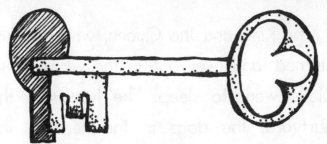

closed door. A rusty old key was in the lock. She turned the key and the door sprang open. There in front of her was an old, bent woman with a spindle, spinning.

'Good day old mother,' said the Princess. 'What are you doing?'

'I am spinning flax, my dear,' said the old woman, nodding her head.

'What sort of thing is that, that rattles around so merrily?' asked the girl, and she took the spindle into her hand, and wanted to spin too. Hardly had she touched the spindle when it pricked her finger, and the spell began to work.

She sank onto the bed that stood there and fell into a deep sleep. Sleep crept over the whole castle.

The King and the Queen, who had just returned, and everyone in the whole court quietly went to sleep. The horses in the courtyard, the dogs in the kennels, the pigeons on the roof, the flies on the wall, even the fire blazing in the hearth slowly settled down to sleep. Outside, the wind fell and the leaves on the trees became still, and a great hush came over everything inside the castle wall.

And round the castle a hedge of thorns began to grow. Every year it got higher until it grew so thick and high that there was nothing left to be seen, not even the flag on the roof.

But the story of the beautiful sleeping Princess was told all through the land. And from time to time Kings' sons from other countries came and tried to push through the thorny hedge into the castle. But the thorns held fast together as if they were hands, and it was impossible for the youths to get through the hedge. And time went by, and even the story of the beautiful sleeping 'Briar-Rose', as she had been called, was almost forgotten.

Many years passed by and another King's son came to the country. He had heard an old man talking about the thorny hedge and about the castle (that some said was lying beneath the thorns) in which a beautiful Princess had been asleep for a hundred years, with the King and Queen and all the court likewise asleep.

His own grandfather had told him that many Princes had come already, and tried to get through the hedge, but had been stopped by the thorns and badly hurt.

The youth said, 'I am not afraid; I will go

and find the beautiful Briar-Rose.' And although his grandfather warned him against it, he did not listen to his words.

When the Prince came near the thorny hedge, he found that it was covered with beautiful flowers. The branches parted for him and let him through without so much as scratching him, and as he went by they closed again behind him.

In the castle yard he saw the horses and the dogs lying asleep, and the pigeons on the roof, their heads tucked under their wings. When he went inside he saw the flies asleep on the walls and the fire only just alight. He went further and he saw the King and the Queen asleep and all the people of the court sleeping also.

Then he walked on further and found the staircase and, as he mounted the stairs, he heard a soft murmur coming from the room where Briar-Rose lay asleep. She looked so young and beautiful that he could not turn his eyes away and he bent down and kissed her. Then Briar-Rose opened her eyes and looked at him, and she smiled as if she had been expecting him. She sat up, and then she and the Prince went down the stairs together.

As they approached, the King and Queen awoke together, and the whole court opened their eyes and looked at each other in astonishment.

The horses in the stables stood up and shook themselves, the dogs jumped up and wagged their tails, the pigeons on the roof lifted their heads from under their wings and flew off to look for food, the flies on the wall began to crawl around, the fire spluttered and began to blaze again, and the cook took the meat off the spit.

The wedding of the Prince and Briar-Rose was celebrated with great rejoicing and they lived happily to the end of their days.

From The Very Naughty
Mother is a Spy
GRETEL KILLEEN

You wouldn't believe it!

One minute the Very Naughty Mother was sitting up in a tree with her children, Zed and Pink, eating their breakfast of fairy floss and honeycomb all wrapped in cheese and ham and chocolate, and the next thing you know a phone rang.

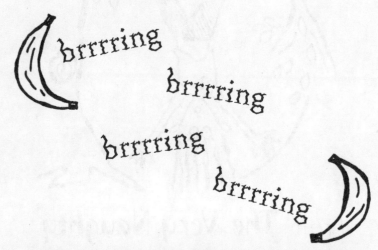

brrrring

brrrring

brrrring

brrrring

So the Very Naughty Mother took the banana from the top left-hand pocket of her polka-dotted pyjamas, and loudly answered the call.

'Hepho,' said the Very Naughty Mother because her mouth was full of fairy floss, honeycomb, cheese, ham and chocolate. 'Hepho. Ith the Vewy Norty Motha here. Canth I helpth u?'

But no one replied, probably because he or she or it or whoever or whatever had rung the banana phone hadn't understood a single word the Very Naughty Mother had said.

So then Zed took the banana phone, because his mother still had her mouth full and pretended to be his mum. 'Hello,' he said in a very high voice just like a squeaky mouse. 'It's the Very Naughty Mother here. Can I help yuuuuuuuuuuuuuuuuuuuuuuu uuuuuuuuuuuuuuuuuuuuuuuuuuuuuuuuuuuuuuuu?'

Well of course the caller still said nothing, and he or she or it or whoever or whatever probably thought they had dialled the wrong number, and he or she or it or whoever or whatever was actually about to hang up, when suddenly Pink took the banana phone. 'Hello,' she said. 'It's the Very Naughty Mother's daughter here, how may I help you?'

And a voice that was louder than a trumpet in your ear bellowed, 'Put the Very Naughty Mother on the banana.'

'Only if you say please,' said Pink as she sat in the tree with her brother and her very naughty mother.

said the voice so angrily that it made the tree shake, and the branches shake, and Zed shake and Pink shake and the Naughty Mother shake, and finally made an egg fall from a wobbling nest up above and land on the Naughty Mother's head.

'It's for you,' said Pink as she handed the banana to her mother, 'and it sounds very much like you are in enormous trouble again.'

'Tell them I'm not here,' said the Very Naughty Mother as she sat on a branch with egg on her head and covered her eyes with her hands.

'No, we won't say that because you *are* here,' said Zed very clearly, 'and so you will answer the banana.'

'But be quick,' said Pink, 'because we're in the middle of our meal and you really shouldn't be talking on the phone even if the phone is something you could also eat.'

So the Very Naughty Mother wiped off the egg that had dribbled from her head onto her ear, took the banana, listened for a moment,

made a face like a possum,

hung up the banana,

and suddenly announced that she had to fly to the Planet of Plopabitofpoop. Immediately.

That's right, she didn't say she had to go to the Planet of Plopabitofpoop tomorrow, or the day after that, or maybe in ten years' time when Grandma and Grandpa had

finished building the space rocket they were making out of an old train carriage and some fireworks. Oh no, no, no, no, no! The Very Naughty Mother said she had to go right now! She had to go right now to Plopabitofpoop!

asked Zed.

'WHAT?'

said Pink. 'What, what, what, what, why?

Why do you have to go to the Planet of Plopabitofpoop, and why do you have to go right now?'

Zed and Pink were a little bit angry. Their breakfasts were often interrupted by their naughty mother's behaviour. Why, only yesterday morning a mermaid had knocked on the door, and last week a crocodile had climbed out of the toilet, and the week before that the Queen had dropped in to stay, and last month four pygmies had popped down the chimney wanting some lemonade. And so Zed and Pink had made a rule last night that there would never be any more interruptions.

'You can't go,' said Pink. 'We're eating our breakfast.'

'But I have to,' said the Very Naughty Mother.

'No,' said Zed. 'You cannot go!'

'Yes I can,' said the Very Naughty Mother

as she gobbled down the rest of her fairy floss and cheese and began to climb down the tree. 'Yes I can go … and you can't stop me.'

'Of course we can stop you,' said Zed and Pink as they grabbed hold of their naughty mother's foot. 'We're stopping you right now!'

'BUT I HAVE TO GO!'

yelled the Very Naughty Mother, wriggling desperately while she tipped over, hung upside down from the tree and struggled to take her foot out of Zed and Pink's clutches.

'No you don't have to go,' said Pink.

'Yes I do so,' said the Very Naughty Mother.

'No you don't,' said Zed.

'Yes I do.'

'No you don't,' said Zed and Pink together.

144

'YES I DO!'

blurted the Very Naughty Mother while she tried to stamp her foot angrily and make a scary thumping sound.

But try as she might to stamp, stamp, stamp, the Very Naughty Mother simply couldn't make a sound because she was still hanging upside down and the only thing she could stamp her foot against was air … and that doesn't make any sound at all. (Okay, maybe a very slight whooshing sound, but absolutely nothing that sounds scary.)

So, as you can imagine, being very angry but only able to make a 'slight whooshing sound' made the Very Naughty Mother even angrier, and so what did the angry Very Naughty Mother do? Did she take a deep breath and calmly explain her situation to Pink and Zed? Well, nearly, but not quite. Because she did take a deep breath, but then ... she actually roared!

'ROO AAAAAAA RRRRRRRR!'

But Zed and Pink were still not scared at all and just continued to hold onto their upside-down mother's feet while Pink asked very gently, 'So why is it that you have to go right now?'

'Because,' gasped the Very Naughty Mother while she tried to hold her breath and sulk at the same time, 'if I don't go right now then ...'

'Yes?' said Pink and Zed.

'Then ...'

'Yes?' said Pink and Zed again.

'Then ...'

'Yes,' said Pink.

'Then ...'

'Hurry up!' said Zed. 'Or we'll soon be one hundred years old and go deaf and never hear the end of the sentence.'

'Well,' said the Very Naughty Mother, 'I have to go right now, or in fact two minutes ago, because I am involved in a race against time to stop ... well, um ... to stop ... well, um ... to stop ...'

'Yes,' panted Zed and Pink, quite breathless with excitement.

'To stop ...'

'To stop what?' said Pink impatiently.

'To stop The Birdies,' whispered the Very Naughty Mother.

'The baddies!' said Zed incredulously. 'Did you just say "to stop the baddies"?'

'No, I said The Birdies. I need to go to the Planet of Plopabitofpoop so that I can stop The Birdies,' mumbled the Very Naughty Mother as she put some spit in the corner of each eye hoping that it would look like tears. Oh, gross!

'Okay, that's enough,' said Zed with a frown. 'I'm really tired of these silly excuses, and this one takes the cake. Why do you have to stop The Birdies? What's the bad thing that they're meant to be doing: singing so loudly it will drive us insane, or just poohing all over the place? We've believed you before when you've told us these tales and not one of them was ever true. Remember when you told us that you couldn't go to work because a smelly slime was going to ooze over the city?

And remember the time you told us you had to buy lollies and hot chips so you could feed them to some invisible  starving friend? And remember that ridiculous time we all had to ride dolphins to the Island of Giggle Ha Ha because you said you were being crowned as their empress?'

'But that one was true,' said the Very Naughty Mother as she sobbed and sobbed upside down and her tears plink-plonked on the basketball that was lying on the grass where she'd left it in the garden last autumn after shooting some goals with the Easter Bunny.

'No, it wasn't true,' said Zed. 'You weren't crowned as the empress, it was just a fancy dress party where you danced around wearing a sheet with tinsel on your head *pretending* that you were a famous empress.'

'Well it was nearly true,' said the Very Naughty Mother very softly as her face began to turn green from hanging upside down for such a long time (which is why we do not recommend that you do it).

'I beg your pardon?' said Pink.

'I said that it was nearly true,' said the Very Naughty Mother even more softly this time.

'I can't hear her,' said Pink to Zed. 'Maybe it's because her head's upside down and her mouth is so far away from our ears.'

'Well we can't bring her back up here, because to get her back up I'd have to let go of her foot and then she might run away,' said Zed.

'Then I'll hold her foot and you hang upside down next to her,' said Pink as she flexed her teeny-weeny muscles.

'No,' said Zed, 'I'll keep holding onto her

and you go upside down to hear what she's
got to say.'

    'No you.'

    'No you.'

    'No you.'

    'No you.'

    'No you.'

    'No you.'

    'No you.'

    'No you.'

    'No you.'

    'No you.'

    'No you.'

'No you.'
'No you.'
'No you.'
'No you.'
'No you.'
'No you.'
'No you.'
'No you.'
'No you.'
'No you.'
'No you.'
'No you.'
'No you.'
'No you.'
'No you.'
'No you.'
'No you.'
'No you.'
'No you.'
'No you.'

'No you.'
'No you.'
'No you.'
'No you.'
'No you.'
'No you.'
'No you.'
'No you.'
'No you.'
'No you.'
'No you.'
'No you.'
'No you.'
'No you.'
'No you.'
'No you.'
'No you.'
'No you.'

'Oh stop arguing and just let go of my feet,'
said the Very Naughty Mother in a voice

that was suddenly loud and clear. *'Why don't you both come down here with me because then we can hang upside down together and it'll be really fantastic.'*

'Oh, now all of a sudden we can hear and understand you!' said Zed who was so angry his face was all twisted and his eyes were popping out. 'What a pity you forgot to continue to whisper, because Pink and I nearly fell for your trick. Oh yes, we nearly both let go of your feet and hung upside down so that we could hear your whispers, but now I'm sure that if we had come down you would have escaped and gone to Plopabitofpoop faster than a supersonic fly.'

'But why would I do that?' said the Very Naughty Mother in a voice as sweet as honey. 'I'm really very happy hanging upside down. It's just like the yoga I learned in Bug-ear from a guru whose name was Roberto.'

'But …' said Pink, feeling quite confused.

'But nothing,' said the Very Naughty Mother. 'All I want to do is hang upside down with my two gorgeous children for the entire day.'

'You're lying again,' said Zed angrily. 'We know that you're trying to fool us.'

'Don't you remember,' interrupted Pink speaking slowly and clearly, 'it was only a few minutes ago that … you … said … you … have … to … go … off … immediately to … save … the … world from birdies?'

'Did I?' mumbled the Very Naughty Mother. 'Oh, I must have forgotten.'

'*You see,*' said Zed, 'it must have all been a lie because you don't just forget something as important as saving the world.'

'Yes, you do if you're hanging upside down,' said the Very Naughty Mother as she tried desperately to think on her feet, even though she was sort of standing on her head. 'You forget everything, big and small, because when you're hanging upside down all of your thoughts and memories tumble straight out your ears.'

'You're trying to trick us,' said Pink with dismay. 'And Zed and I have had enough. You should go to your room and stay there all day and tonight have no dessert. And that will be really, really bad because tonight

we're serving your *favourite* desert, the fabulous chocolate-puff-puff-pert,' (which is a cake made out of chocolate, chocolate, chocolate and chocolate and then smothered with chocolate sauce).

And so it was decided that the Very Naughty Mother was to be sent to her room without any dessert and the door would be shut tight so she couldn't run away. And once this was agreed, Zed clapped his hands to sort of say 'hurry up'. And he accidentally let go of the naughty mother's foot.

Oh yes, that's right, the Naughty Mother's foot fell from Zed's grasp, and because she was heavy she also slid through Pink's fingers, and then the Very Naughty Mother ...

FELL, FELL, FELL, FELL,

hardly any distance at all and landed on the basketball that I mentioned before that was sitting in the lawn right underneath the branch where they'd all been eating breakfast.

But the Very Naughty Mother wasn't on the basketball for long, because perhaps a squincy-second after landing on it she bounced, boi-oi-oing off the basketball and up into the sky.

Higher

and higher

and higher

and higher she boinged,

past hovering insects

past swooping birds

past clumps of clouds

 past the sizzling sun

and all the way up to the moon.

Oh yes, it's true. The Very Naughty Mother flew very, very high up into the sky, and strangely enough she could have actually reached the Planet of Plopabitofpoop. Well, she could have if she hadn't got greedy and grabbed a huge piece of cheese when she boinged past the moon ...

because the weight of such a huge piece of cheese made her start to fall,

fall,
fall,
fall,
all the way back down to Earth.
So, she fell past the twinkling stars
and past the swirling rainbow
and past the hovering mosquitoes
and past the tree where Zed and Pink
were standing with their mouths wide open
in amazement,

and she even fell past the basketball.

Well, actually, not so much 'past the basketball', but 'next to the basketball'.

Well no, she didn't actually fall 'past the basketball' or 'next to the basketball', because to be more precise she sort of fell *near* the basketball,

but not that near to it, because the basketball was on the lawn, and the Very Naughty Mother landed in the sandpit.

Anyway, I think you get the idea, that one minute the Very Naughty Mother was going up, up, up and the next minute she was going down, DOWN, DOWN, DOWN, DOWN,

until she landed with
a kerthump,
squish,
splat,
kerplop,
right in the middle of the sandpit.

And that my friends is where the Very Naughty Mother suddenly yelled. 'Help, help, I'm sinking in the sandpit. The sandpit has turned into quicksand.'

To be continued ...

From **The Cockroach Cup**

KIM CARAHER

1

I got into this mess because I couldn't keep my big mouth shut.

It all started when Max brought a tightly tied-up shoebox to school.

'What's in there, Max?' I asked.

'You'll see,' he said. 'When I'm good and ready.'

'Of course, everybody wanted to know after that. You couldn't see Max for the crowd. He wouldn't say a thing, but everybody else was very noisy. Ms Grabble got annoyed.

'Take that box outside, Max,' she said. 'The rest of you, sit down.'

Max took the box out.

Not much later, he asked to go to the toilet. As he disappeared there was a rush of excuses from other people wanting to go too. Ms Grabble ignored most of them, but she let Sarah go. She reckons Sarah is sensible and trustworthy.

A few seconds later, Sarah's scream rattled the windows. We all tried to squeeze through the door at once to see what had happened. Max was sitting on a bench outside the classroom. Sarah was running round and round his box.

'Oh yuk, it's horrible! They are horrible!' she was yelling. She had a big smile on her face. 'Yuk, yuk, yuk!'

'Stop it, Sarah,' said Ms Grabble. 'Both of you, come inside at once. Max, bring that box.'

'But Miss —' said Max.

'At once, Max!' said Ms Grabble.

They came in.

'Okay, Max, what's in the box?' said Ms Grabble.

Max just stared at the floor, and muttered.

This was when Ms Grabble made her big mistake. 'Give me the box, Max,' she said, and leaned over to take it. There was a sort of fumble-pass. The box fell.

Cockroaches started running everywhere.

Big ones, little ones, brown ones, black ones, flying ones and an incredibly huge, mouse-sized one.

Kids scattered in all directions. Some jumped on top of desks. I jumped down and started stamping. I was just about to stamp on the mouse-sized monster when Max threw himself in front of me.

It wasn't my fault I stamped on his hand instead.

Max's screaming was worse than the screams of all the rest of the kids put together. First he screamed on and on about his broken hand. Then he started screaming that I'd murdered Michelangelo. But it wasn't my foot that squashed the thing. It was Max's hand. I could clearly see the spattered remains of giant cockroach all over it.

I was kind of glad it wasn't all over my foot.

'Murderer!' yelled Max. 'I'm going to report you to the RSPCA.'

'Oh come off it, Max,' I said. 'It was only a cockroach.'

'Only a cockroach! Only a cockroach! It was my champion! There has never been a cockroach like Michelangelo! And there never will be again.'

He was practically in tears.

'I've seen hundreds of cockroaches like that. There must be thousands, millions, billions!' I said. And that's when I opened my mouth wide enough to put my foot in it. 'I could find a better cockroach than that any day!'

'Oh, could you?' said Max. 'Well, do it!'

'What?'

'Find one and we'll have a race. On Monday, at recess. Your can race against Daisy: she's my second best.'

He glared at me and patted his top pocket. I could just see Daisy's little feelers poking out and waving.

'I suppose she's my first best now. At least I managed to save her from your big feet. You don't stand a chance.'

Actually, I agreed with him. I wouldn't stand a chance against someone who could tell boy cockroaches from girl cockroaches.

But once I've said something, I stick to it.

Somehow I had to find a champion cockroach ...

4

Beep, bee-eep.

Beep, bee-eep.

Beep, bee-eep-eep-eep —

My mind just knew it wasn't time to get up. I turned over. But the noise wouldn't go away.

'Emma! Emma!' Now it was [my friend] Cathy's voice. 'Time to go hunting!'

I opened my eyes. 'Oh, go away, Cathy. I'll do it tomorrow.'

'Emma! You wake up this minute, or … I'll catch all the cockroaches myself and tuck them into bed with you!'

Once I sat up, I didn't feel so bad. I looked at the clock. Two am. Some of the excitement of the chase started to well up in me.

'Have you got the torch?'

Cathy shone it in my face.

'Okay, okay. Turn it off. Let's go.'

It was dark in the kitchen. It was quiet, but it wasn't silent. Listening carefully, we could hear the tiny scuttle of hundreds of little legs, busily creeping and crawling, doing whatever it is that cockroaches do in the dead of night.

I switched on the torch, shining it on the shelf next to the cassettes. About half a dozen cockroaches froze in the beam. On the edges of the light, there was a general scampering and scuttling for cover.

'Put the cups over the biggest ones,' I hissed. 'Quick!'

Cathy was quick. She covered two of the biggies, but the third got away. I looked after it sadly.

'Now, that one would have been a champion! Look how fast it moved. That's the trouble with all these plans. We only catch the ones that aren't fast. What's the good of that?'

'Stop whingeing and help me get these two into the box,' said Cathy.

As she lifted the cup, one started to run out. She plonked the cup down again quickly. Not quite over the cockroach. More like on top of it.

'You've chopped it in half!'

'Okay, so you do it!'

So I carefully scooped the one cockroach we had left into the box. It looked kind of lonely and pathetic, scurrying about waving its feelers. It didn't look like much of a champion. Not much of a match for Daisy at all. I dropped a bit of sugar into the box to start building it up. Then I snapped the lid.

We crept back to bed. It took me ages to fall asleep, and when I did, all I dreamt about were crowds of giant cockroaches racing camels round the schoolyard.

5

'We need to give it a name,' I said to Cathy the next morning. 'So we can encourage it properly.'

'Is it a boy or a girl?' asked Cathy.

I gave her a withering look. 'Who cares?' I said. 'We'll call it Cool. Cool, the cockroach. And we'll say it's a boy, 'cause Daisy's a girl. Come on Cool: time to start training.'

Have you ever tried to train a cockroach? It's not easy, I'm telling you.

6

As soon as we arrived at school, kids were crowding round us, wanting to see Cool.

'What's all this?' I asked Cathy. 'I didn't think so many people would be interested.'

Then we saw it. Just next to the bike shed, there was a big banner.

Sitting under the banner was Ricky, our class maths whiz. He had two sheets of paper: one with DAISY written across the top, and a few names; the other was blank. He had a little pile of money in front of him already.

'What do you think you're doing, Ricky?' I asked.

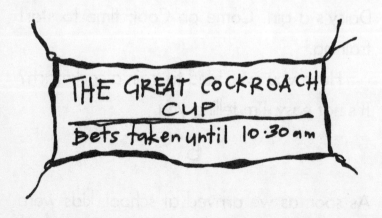

'What does it look like?'

He always answers a question with another question.

'You'd better let me see your cockroach, so I can give out the odds. So far, all the bets are on Daisy to win.'

'How can anyone bet on Daisy? They haven't even seen Cool yet! He's the fastest cockroach in the universe!'

'COOL,' Ricky wrote on the other sheet. 'Good name. Well, come on, then let's see him.'

'No way,' I said. 'He's a secret weapon. Everyone will see him at recess time and that's it!'

7

At recess, we had to fight our way onto the basketball court through the crowd that had come to see the race. ...

Max had drawn a circle on the bitumen.

'Come on, Cool,' I whispered to the box. 'It's your big moment.'

Max and I headed for the centre of the circle.

'DAI-SY! DAI-SY! DAI-SY!' a few of them started to chant, and it grew.

'COO-OOL, COO-OOL, COO-OOL!' shouted Cathy in return. At first she was the only one. Then more joined in.

'On your marks, get set, go! said Ricky. We tipped them out.

8

Daisy headed straight for the edge.

And Cool froze. I couldn't believe it. The stupid insect didn't move at all. Daisy was zooming to the finish line.

'DAI-SY! DAI-SY! DAI-SY!'

The yell was even more deafening than the rain on a metal roof.

'What's wrong, Cool, broken a leg — or six?' shouted one of Max's supporters.

It felt like time was standing still as Daisy got closer and closer to the finish line and my stupid 'champion' hadn't moved a millimetre. Max was laughing and screaming.

This was the worst moment of my life. Here I was, standing in the middle of a circle with everyone laughing at me and a cockroach who might as well be dead. Maybe he was dead.

Then Daisy stopped. She was about a centimetre from the finish line, but she just stopped.

She turned round. She started to walk, slowly, back to the centre of the circle. There was a silence, then a cheer from Cool's supporters.

'Come on, Daisy, turn!' yelled Max.

But Daisy kept going, back to the centre of the circle.

Then it hit me. She wasn't interested in finishing the race. She was interested in Cool. She was going to eat him!

Maybe Cool had worked out the same thing, because just as Daisy's feelers were about to touch him, he suddenly turned, and ran.

He ran straight, and fast. Daisy was taken by surprise. She was miles behind. Cool ran straight over the finish line.

There was a massive cheer.

He'd won the Cockroach Cup! ...

To be continued ...

MARGARET CLARK is one of Australia's most popular writers for young people. She has worked as a teacher and university lecturer and at the Geelong Centre for Alcohol and Drug Dependency. Her novels for older readers include, *The Big Chocolate Bar*, *Fat Chance*, *Hot or What*, *Kiss and Make Up*, *Famous for Five Minutes* and a trilogy about the Studley family: *Hold my Hand or Else!*, *Living with Leanne* and *Pulling the Moves*. *Back on Track: Diary of a Streetkid*, *No Standing Zone*, *Care Factor Zero*, and *Bad Girl*, four searing novels for young adults, have become bestsellers. Most recently her *Secret Girls' Stuff*, *More Secret Girls' Stuff*, and *What to do When Life Sucks* have been hits with her many fans.

DUNCAN BALL was born in the United States and then moved around a lot with his family before coming to Sydney in 1974. He began work as an industrial chemist but he soon decided he wanted to fulfil his original dream of becoming a writer and began writing for both adults and children. Duncan is best known as the creator of the *Selby the Talking Dog* series, beginning with *Selby's Secret*. His other books include the *Emily Eyefinger* series, the *Ghost of the Gory* series and a number of books in the *Case Of* series.

MALORIE BLACKMAN worked as a database manager and systems programmer before becoming a full-time writer. Her reputation has steadily grown and she has been awarded a number of prizes including the WH Smith's Mind-Boggling Books Award and the Young Telegraph/ Gimme 5 award for *HACKER*, the Young Telegraph/ Fully Booked award for

THIEF! and, more recently, shortlisted for the Carnegie Medal.

JENNY WAGNER lives in a small Queensland farmhouse that looks like a witch's cottage. Jenny likes writing best of all, unless it's going badly, in which case she hates it. She also likes going for walks, listening to classical music, studying languages, getting together with friends and putting off the vacuuming. As well as her best-selling novels featuring the Nimbin, Jenny has also written children's picture books: *The Bunyip of Berkeley's Creek* and *John Brown, Rose and the Midnight Cat* both won CBC Book of the Year Awards and are widely considered to be classics.

JOAN AIKEN came from a family of writers; daughter of the American poet, Conrad Aiken, her sister Jane also wrote novels. Joan Aiken wrote over a hundred books for young readers and adults. Her best-known books are those in the *James III* saga of which the classic *The Wolves of Willoughby Chase* was the first title, published in 1962 and awarded the Lewis Carroll prize. Both that and *Black Hearts in Battersea* were filmed. Her books are internationally acclaimed and she received the Edgar Allan Poe Award in the United States as well as the Guardian Award for Fiction for *The Whispering Mountain*. She was decorated with the MBE for her services

to children's books. Her last book, *The Witch of Clatteringshaws*, was published in 2005.

ANNA FIENBERG is a storyteller much loved for her works of fantasy and magic. She grew up in a house filled with books and started writing stories when she was eight, but never imagined being an author. 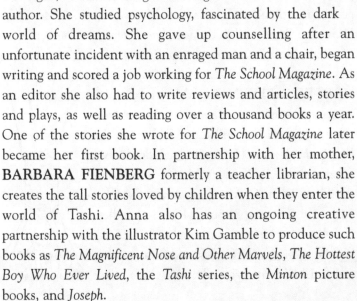 She studied psychology, fascinated by the dark world of dreams. She gave up counselling after an unfortunate incident with an enraged man and a chair, began writing and scored a job working for *The School Magazine*. As an editor she also had to write reviews and articles, stories and plays, as well as reading over a thousand books a year. One of the stories she wrote for *The School Magazine* later became her first book. In partnership with her mother, **BARBARA FIENBERG** formerly a teacher librarian, she creates the tall stories loved by children when they enter the world of Tashi. Anna also has an ongoing creative partnership with the illustrator Kim Gamble to produce such books as *The Magnificent Nose and Other Marvels*, *The Hottest Boy Who Ever Lived*, the *Tashi* series, the *Minton* picture books, and *Joseph*.

VICTOR KELLEHER was born in London in 1939 and came to Australia in 1976 after living in South Africa and New Zealand. Victor's books have won and been shortlisted for many awards, including the Children's Book Council of Australia Book of the Year Award. His books include *Master of the Grove* (1982), *Taronga* (1986), *Beyond the Dusk* (2000) and the *Goblin* series. He now writes both children's and adult's novels full-time from his home in Bellingen, New South Wales.

CLARE SCOTT-MITCHELL had a long career teaching Children's Literature to tertiary students, in particular, at the Institute of Early Childhood, Macquarie University. She collaborated with Richard Gill on many music projects, particularly operas, for children and young people. Her poetry anthologies *When a Goose Meets a Moose*, *Apples From Hurricane Street* and *100 Australian Poems for Children* were seminal points in Australian publishing for children.

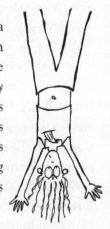

GRETEL KILLEEN started her career as a stand-up comic. She appears regularly on national television and radio and hosts the *Big Brother* shows. Her books include the *My Sister's* and *Very Naughty Mother* series, plus the Fleur Trotter – *My Life* – series. Gretel is currently running around like a headless chook raising her son and daughter, preparing several of her works for TV and film, and has just finished writing an adult novel.

KIM CARAHER loves writing books for children because it's fun. She loves dreaming things up, and then making them happen in a story. She lives in Darwin with her family, which includes some Electronic Life Forms disguised as children. They have told her it can be dangerous, even fatal, to make Electronic Life Forms switch off a game when they are about to reach the next level. Especially to do homework. Kim wrote *The Cockroach Cup* and *Zip Zap* for Random House.

ABOUT THE EDITOR

Linsay Knight is widely respected as a leading expert in, and contributor to, children's literature in Australia. As the Head of Children's Books at Random House Australia, Linsay has nurtured the talent of numerous authors and illustrators to create some of Australia's most successful children's books. Linsay is also the author of several successful non-fiction children's books, and the editor of 30 *Australian Stories for Children* and 30 *Australian Ghost Stories for Children* for Random House Australia.

ABOUT THE ILLUSTRATOR

Jobi Murphy is a freelance designer and illustrator who has worked on numerous books for Random House including *Muddled Up Farm*, *Max Remy: Superspy*, *The Saddle Club*, *Pony Tails* and the *Vidz* series. She was also responsible for designing Blake Education's award-winning *My Alphabet Kit*.

Despite being discouraged from mixing her colours by her second-grade teacher, Jobi fulfilled a long-time ambition when she began working in children's publishing. She now divides her time between illustrating and designing children's books, and enjoying time with her husband and baby son in the bushy Sydney suburb of Grays Point.

ACKNOWLEDGEMENTS

1 *The Biggest Boast* by Margaret Clark reprinted by permission of Random House Australia Pty Ltd. Text Copyright © Margaret Clark 1995.

2 Extract from *Emily Eyefinger and the Ghost Ship*, 'Emily and the Missing Pets', by Duncan Ball reprinted by permission of Harper Collins Publishers. Text copyright © Duncan Ball 2004.

3 *The Old Duppy's Curse or How I was Turned into a Crocodile* by Malorie Blackman reprinted by permission of A.M. Heath and Co Ltd. First published in *A Stack of Story Poems* collected by Tony Bradman, Doubleday 1992. Text copyright © Oneta Malorie Blackman 1992.

4 *The Werewolf Knight* by Jenny Wagner reprinted by permission of Random House Australia. Published by Random House 1995.Text Copyright © Jenny Wagner 1987.

5 *The Patchwork Quilt* by Joan Aiken reprinted by permission of A.M. Heath and Co Ltd. First published in A *Necklace of Rainbows*, Jonathan Cape 1968. Text copyright © Joan Aiken Enterprises Ltd 1968.

6 Extract from *The Big, Big Book of Tashi*, 'Tashi and the Giants', by Anna and Barbara Fienberg, reprinted by permission of Allen & Unwin. Text Copyright © Anna and Barbara Fienberg 1996.

7 *Goblin in the Bush* by Victor Kelleher reprinted by permission of Random Australia Pty Ltd. Text Copyright © Victor Kelleher 2002.

8 *Sleeping Beauty* retold by Clare Scott-Mitchell reprinted by permission of Random House Australia Pty Ltd. Text Copyright © Clare Scott-Mitchell 2000.

9 Extract from *The Very Naughty Mother is a Spy* by Gretel Killeen reprinted by permission of Random House Australia Pty Ltd. Text Copyright © Gretel Killeen 2004.

10 Extract from *The Cockroach Cup* by Kim Caraher reprinted by permission of Random House Australia Pty Ltd. Text Copyright © Kim Caraher 1998.